PUFFI'
Editor:

GW0085732?

MY AUNT

Charlotte Hough has compiled, written and illustr...
a real 'nothing-like-it-before' book, which combines
usefulness with bright colour and a hilarious joyfulness
with a word and picture appeal which no young child
(reader or non-reader) will be able to resist.

My Aunt's Alphabet, then, is the first and last and
most lighthearted word for alphabetarians, a primer of
logical spelling. It will cleverly lure into the world of
Billy and 'me', Dan the dog and Izzy, the cat and the
hen who hurried away with the handy hat on her head,
every reluctant and every enthusiastic reader. (And,
please note, for the parentally deprived, no mother or
father makes an appearance – just a substantially
reassuring aunt, who appears with welcome frequency.)

My Aunt's Alphabet

with Billy and Me

by Charlotte Hough

Penguin Books

Penguin Books Ltd, Harmondsworth, Middlesex, England
Penguin Books Inc. 7110 Ambassador Road, Baltimore, Maryland 21207, U.S.A.
Penguin Books Australia Ltd, Ringwood, Victoria, Australia

First published by Hamish Hamilton and Penguin Books 1969
Reprinted by Penguin Books 1970
Copyright © Charlotte Hough, 1969
Made and printed in Great Britain
by H. L. Vickery Ltd, Hackbridge, Surrey

To Margaret Joseph, who can make
anybody read

NOTE

Compounds used in this book:

AR	as in FAR	OR	as in FOR
AY	as in AWAY	OU	as in OUT
CH	as in SUCH	SH	as in DASH
CK	as in QUICK	TH	as in THIS
EE	as in SEE	WH	as in WHEN
ER	as in CLEVER		
ING	as in SITTING		
LE	as in MUDDLE		
NK	as in INK		
OO	as in ROOM		

LOOK-SAY WORDS

There are 280 words in this book, listed at the back. Where the pronunciation is not quite logical, such as in THE, they are indicated in colour. These are kept to a minimum, but just have to be learned by looking at them.

I have included the final E here, as in FIVE, because although it *is* logical, it is rather difficult.

As well as my aunt
you will see us in this book

Me

Billy

The cat

Dan
with
Izzy

A grub

A
tom-tit

A
hen

A
zebra

he
rrot

5
fish

A a

This is

my aunt.

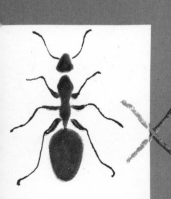

Not an

ant.

I am bad at sums so I ask her to add them up for me.

It is a pity she has a cold.

ATISHOO!

B b

When I did my sums
Billy hit me with my
big bat. Bonk!

My aunt sent
him to bed,
but he
bit her.

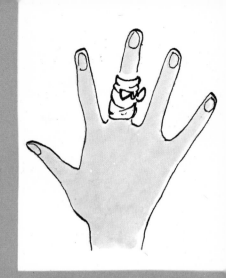

He can be a
bad baby.

C c

Clever Billy can carry the cat.

He puts her in his cot

so she will not be

cold and feeds her

with a crust. She is

cosy but may soon

get cross.

D d

My aunt is fond of her
dog Dan. We dash about
with him.
When he dug
deeply Billy got dusty,

He may

cry!

No,
big boys
don't cry.

E e

Billy has upset his egg.
"You have had eleven
eggs and upset them every
time!" said my aunt.

" This is the **end!** "

But

Billy is

happy.

He is

not fond

of **eggs**

F f

I felt for a fish in the pond.

It is full of fat fish.
They flap their fins and
I can feel five.

They feel funny!

G g

Billy has dug up a
grey grub in the mud,
and has it in his hand.

"Goodness, get that grub!"
gasps my aunt.
　　　But Billy drops it in
the green grass.

Go away grub. Good-bye.

H h

This (hat) was (handy) so
Billy put it on a (hen).

" (Help ! Here) is my aunt! "

Hallo! she says, "have
you seen my hat?"
"Yes, but hurry, it is
running up the hill!"

"That's funny," says my
aunt, "but never mind,
it was a horrid hat."

I i

This is my Indian, Izzy.
He is dusty and inky but
I am fond of him.

Izzy is ill so I put him into bed. I think

he has my aunt's cold.

He says he feels itchy.

J j

As Izzy is ill he has a jab with a pin so he will soon be well.

He is jolly good and didn't
cry so I have just given him

a jelly.

K k

I am big so I am King.

I am a kind king, not a
horrid king, so I won't
kill you.   I will keep you
happy and if you cry I
will kiss you better.

L l

Izzy is lazy. Look, he
won't stand up! His
left leg is funny.

Dan bit it and it lost

a lot of stuffing.

Let Dan lick him so

he will soon be better.

Good luck, Izzy!

M m

My aunt is in a bad mood.
Billy has muddled all her maps

Dan is muddy and the milk is spilt so that the middle of

the room is all messy.

She must mop it up.

N n

The cat is having a nap.

No, you must not nip her

nose, Dan . . .

...nor her neck! That is never a kind thing to do.

Whatever next!

Izzy can stand on that odd leg!

My kind aunt has mended it
and it is O.K.

He often needs mending.
If only Dan was good!
It is a pity he is such
a bad old dog.

P p

Polly

is

a

pet parrot.

I pat Dan but she
often pecks him.
I think she is a pest

but she is also pretty,
so that is lucky.

Q q

I am very fond of the Queen.

She is not far away and I
can run quickly to help her,

but she has not
needed me yet.

R r

Dan has left a grey rat
on the red rug.

" Get rid of it! " begs
my aunt. She has run
quickly from the room.

That was rotten of
Dan and bad luck
on my aunt.

S s

I saw Dan dig up the sand-pit.

He was looking for his stick.

I didn't stop him, so I
was sent away.

I am sitting on the steps
in the sun, very sulky.
It is sad.

But the cat is kind to me.

T t

The cat took a tuft
from the tail of
a tom-tit.

That was a bad trick so
I tugged her tail,
too.

I'm glad that tom-tit
got away.

U u

My uncle often tucks us up in bed with a kiss.

He thinks he is ugly, but
he is not at all, nor
is he ever unkind.

He is just untidy.

We think he is super.

V v

I don't need a **vest**.

It feels **very** silly.

My aunt says I must
have a vest when I visit
her, and that I am
only vain.

I am sulky.
I bet my aunt has no vest.

W w

We went to a wedding
with my aunt,

and it was very wet and
windy.
    She wore a red wool hat
but the wind took it

away over the hill.

X x

Have you

ever had

an

 X-ray ?

I have and it is

not bad.

I fell out of a tree and

my aunt ran quickly to

help me.

The X-ray said I was O.K.

Y y

Polly is green.   Not 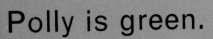yellow.

She yells much too much.
"Yes, you are a silly parrot!"
says my aunt. But she
cannot stop her yet.

Soon we may all go mad.

Z z

Billy's zip got stuck when
he went to the zoo. It had
a bit of bun in the middle.

My aunt mended the zip and a zebra took the buns.

My aunt is clever and her cold is better.

INDEX

A

a
about
add
all
also
am
an
and
ant
are
as
ask
at
atishoo
aunt
away

B

baby
bad
bat
be
bed
begs
bet
better
big
Billy
bit
bonk!

book
boys
bun
but

C

can
cannot
carry
cat
clever
cold
cosy
cot
cross
crust
cry

D

Dan
dash
deeply
did
didn't
dig
dog
don't
drops
dug
dusty

E

egg
eleven
end
ever
every

F

fat
far
feeds
feel
fell
felt
fins
fish
five
flap
fond
for
from
full
funny

G

gasps
get
given
glad

go
good
good-bye
goodness!
got
grass
green
grey
grub

H

had
hallo
hand
handy
happy
has
hat
have
having
he
hen
help
her
here
hill
him
his
hit
horrid
hurry

I

I
if
ill
I'm
in
Indian
inky
into
is
it
itchy
Izzy

J

jab
jam
jelly
jolly
just

K

keep
kill
kind
king
kiss

L

lazy
left

leg
let
lick
look
looking
lost
lot
luck
lucky

M

mad
maps
may
me
mended
mending
messy
middle
milk
mind
mood
mop
much
mud
muddled
muddy
must
my

N

nap
neck
need
needed
needs
never
next
nip
no
nor
nose
not

O

odd
of
often
O.K.
old
on
only
or
out
over

P

parrot
pat
pecks
pest
pet

pin
pity
Polly
pond
pretty
put

Q

Queen
quickly

R

ran
rat
red
rid
room
rotten
rug
run
running

S

sad
said
sand-pit
saw
says
see
seen
sent
she
silly

sitting
so
soon
stand
steps
stick
stop
stuffing
spilt
such
sulky
sums
sun
super

T

tail
that
the
their
them
they
thing
think
this
time
to
tom-tit
too
took
tree
trick
tucks

tuft
tugged

U

ugly
uncle
unkind
us
untidy
up

V

vain
very
vest
visit

W

was
we
wedding
well
went
wet
will
wind
windy
with
whatever
when
won't
wool
wore

X

X-ray

Y

yellow
yells
yes
yet
you

Z

zebra
zip
zoo